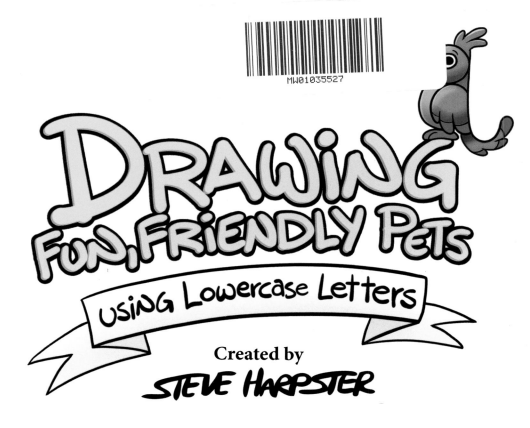

DRAWING
FUN, FRIENDLY PETS
using Lowercase Letters

Created by
STEVE HARPSTER

HARPTOONS™ PUBLISHING

www.harptoons.com

Thanks to my creative and wonderful
son Tyler who came up with the idea for
this book! Love you buddy.

Library of Congress Cataloging-in-Publication Data
Library of Congress Control Number: 2015901897
Harpster, Steve
Drawing Fun, Friendly Pets Using Lowercase Letters
written and illustrated by Steve Harpster

SUMMARY: Learn how to draw pets by starting with a lowercase letter
ART / General, JUVENILE FICTION / General

ISBN: 978-0-9960197-1-2
ISBN: 0-9960197-1-5

SAN: 859-6921

**For school visits and art programs please go to www.harptoons.com
or contact Steve Harpster by email at steve@harptoons.com**

Follow Harptoons on:

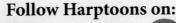

Welcome to *Drawing Fun, Friendly Pets Using Lowercase Letters*. The goal of this book is to make drawing easy and fun! On some of the pages you might see an icon like this...

Watch Steve draw this at
HARPTOONS™.com

This means I have a video of me drawing this pet at Harptoons.com. So grab your pencil and some paper and turn on your imagination, and let's draw fun, friendly pets.

Happy Drawing,

STEVE HARPSTER

Watch Steve draw this at
HOOTOONS.com

Dogs and Puppies

Dogs and Puppies

TRY DRAWING THESE DOGS.

Dogs and Puppies

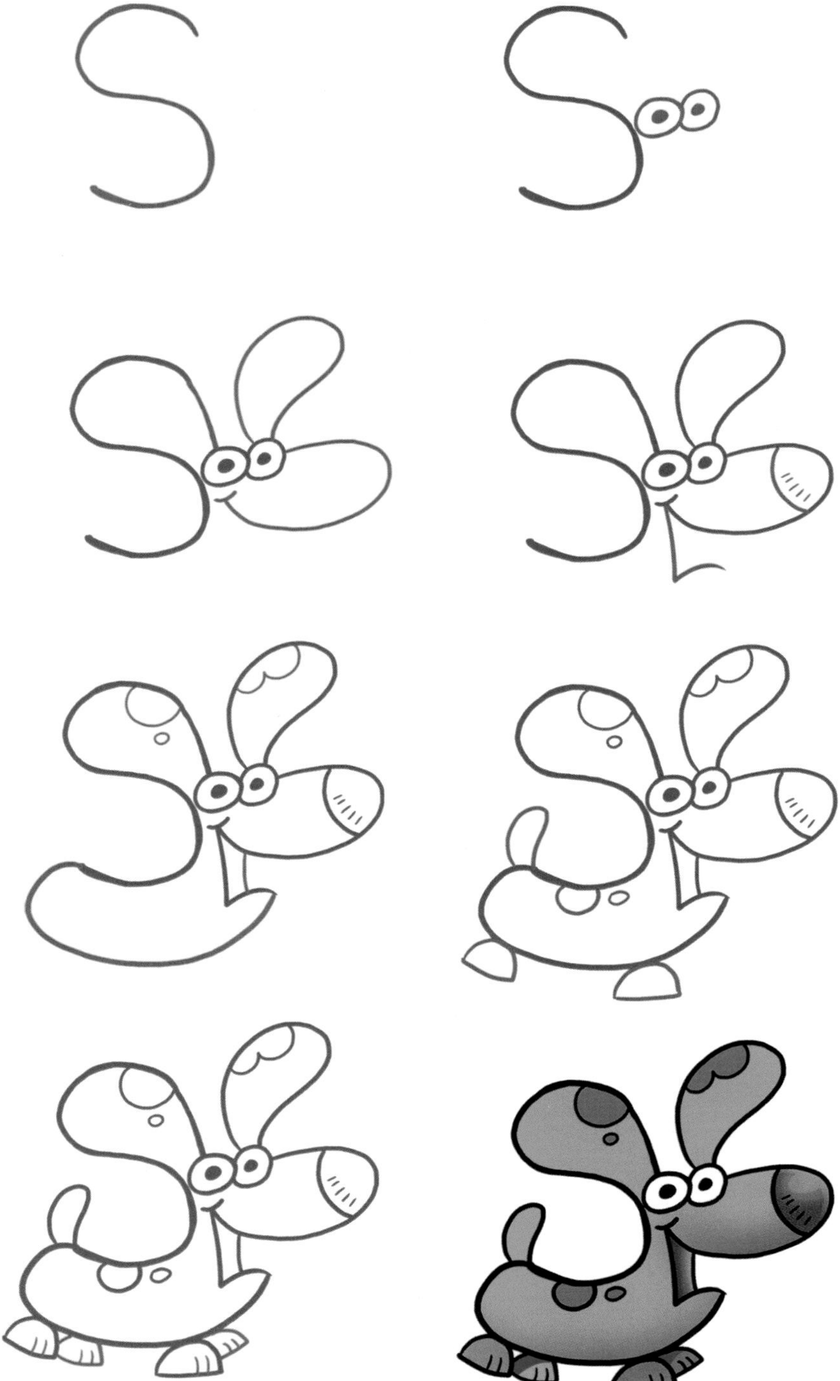

Dogs and Puppies

TRY DRAWING THESE DOGS.

CATS and KITTENS

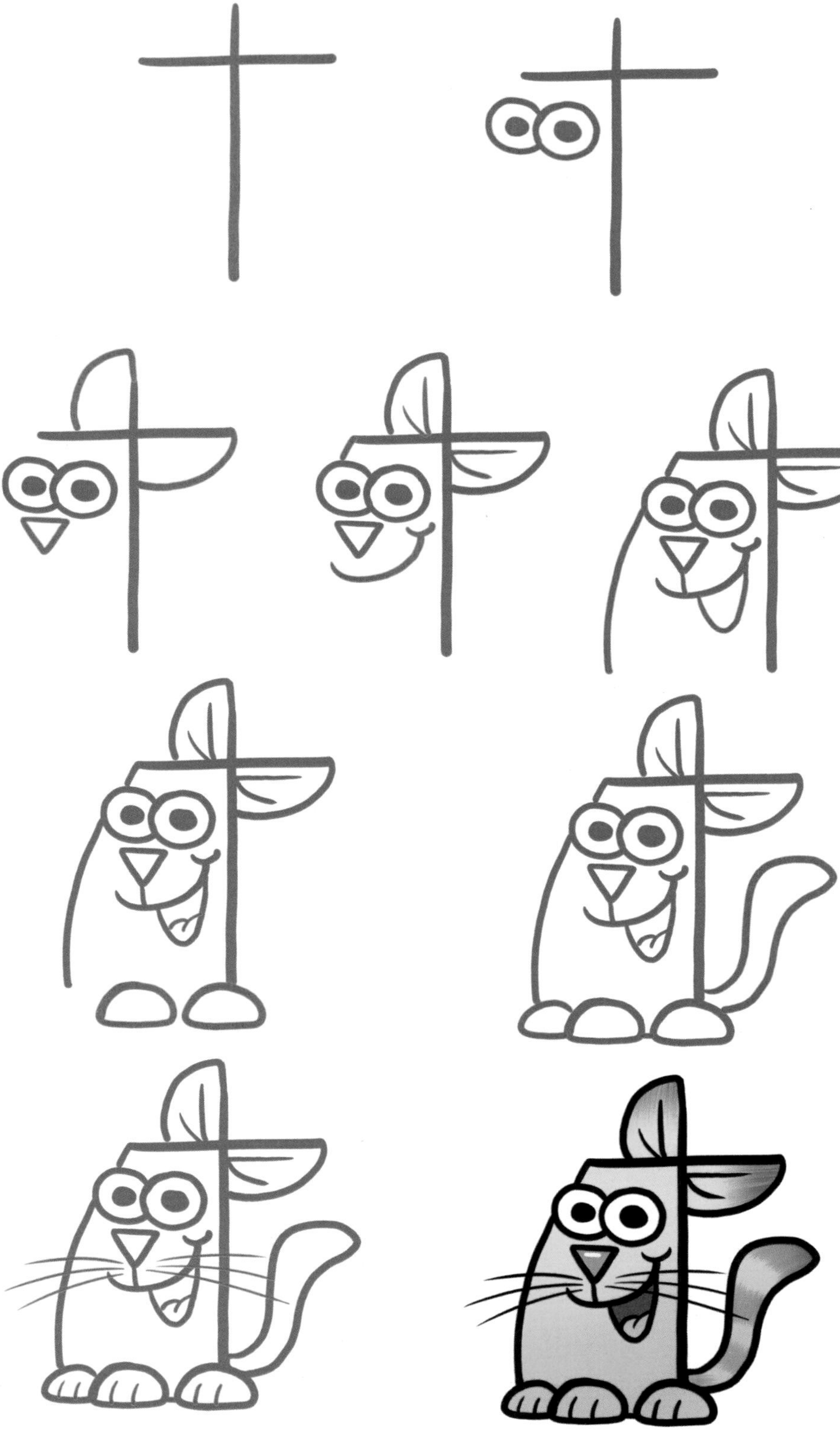

Watch Steve draw this at
HARPTOONS.com

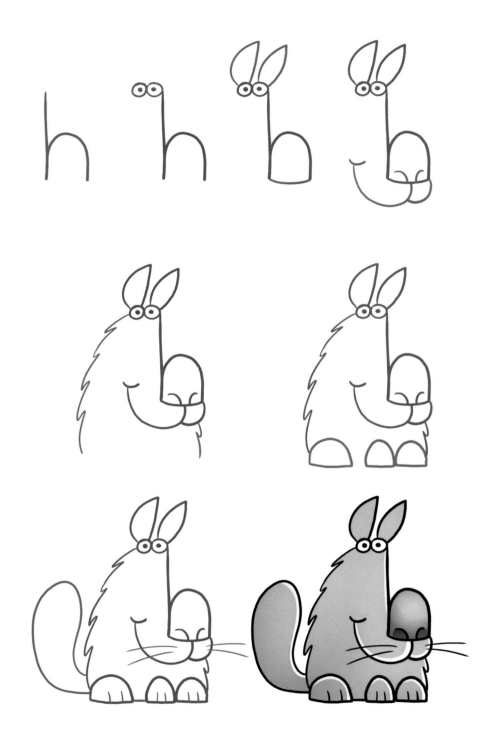

guinea pig

TRY CREATING ALL KINDS OF
FUN LOOKING GUINEA PIGS.

Small Furry Pets

dwarf hamster

gerbil

mouse

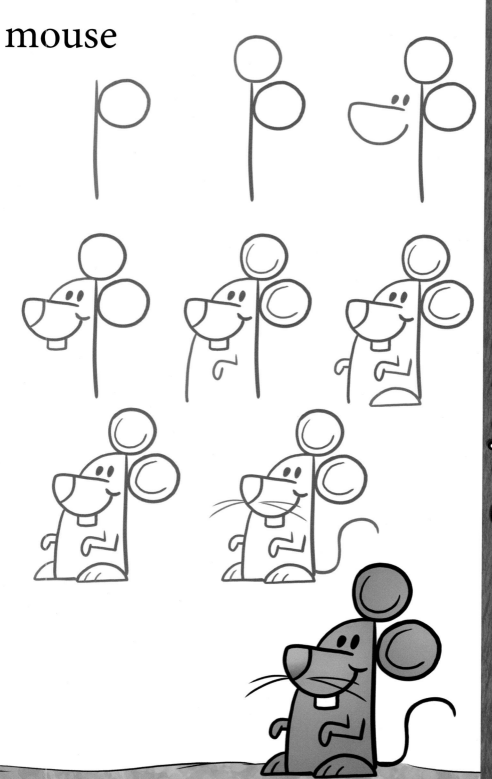

bunny

ferret

turtle

bearded dragon

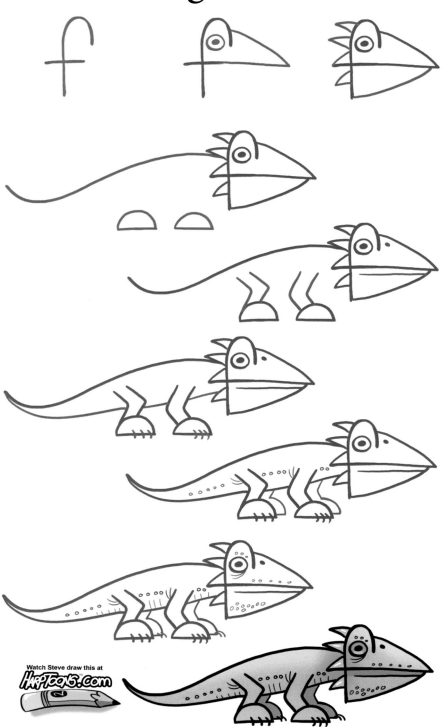

REPTILES AND AMPHIBIANS

newt

iguana

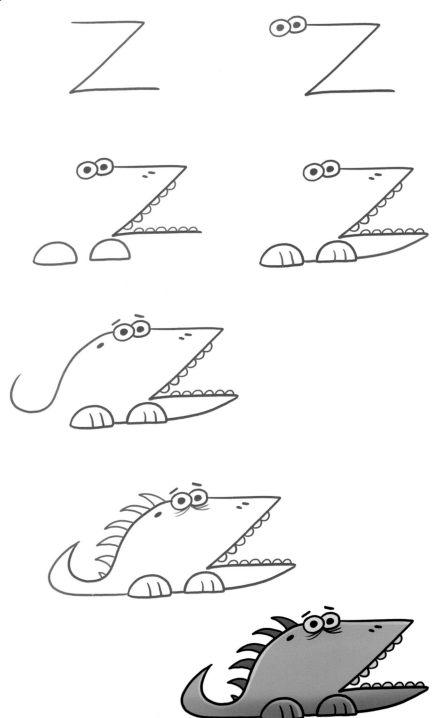

snake

chameleon

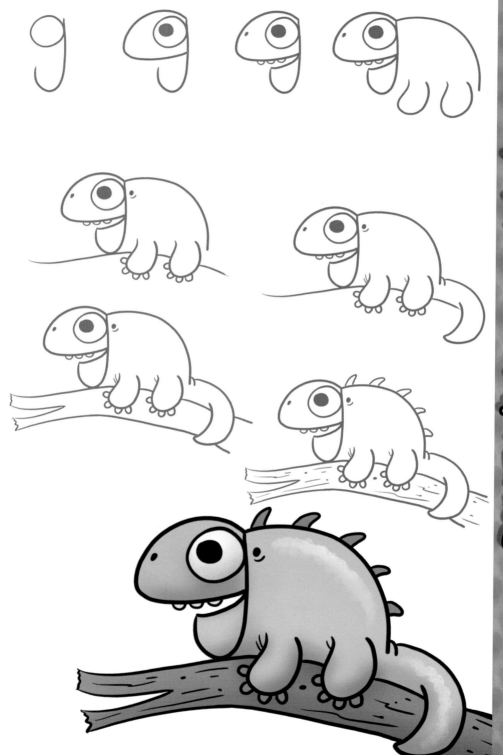

frog

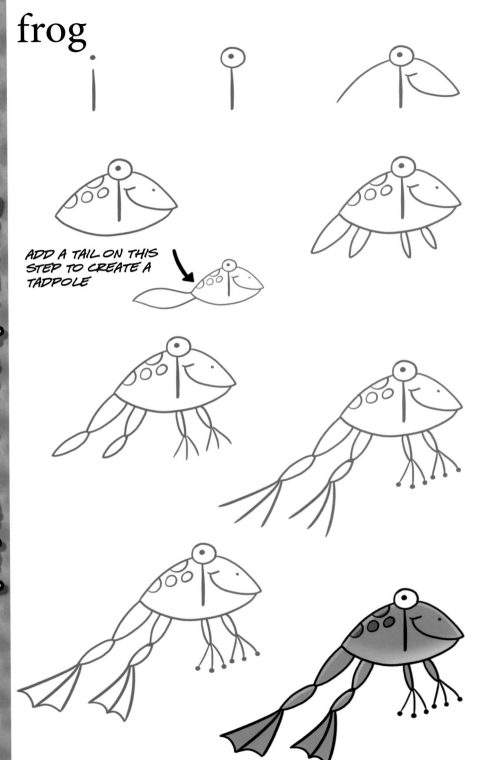

ADD A TAIL ON THIS STEP TO CREATE A TADPOLE

snail

seahorse

fish

fish

parakeet

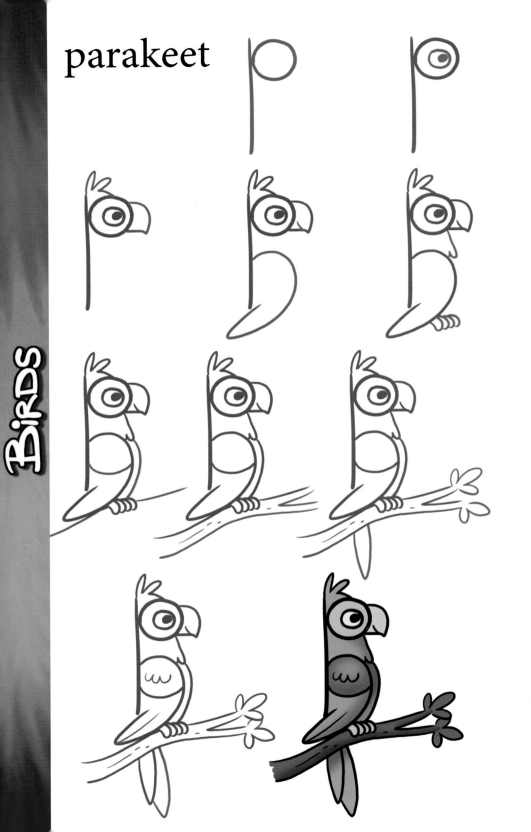

finch

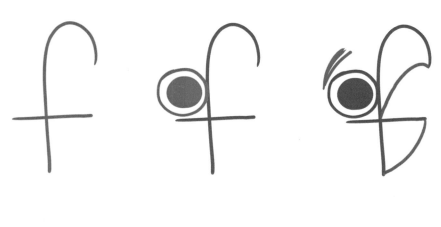

parrot

tarantula

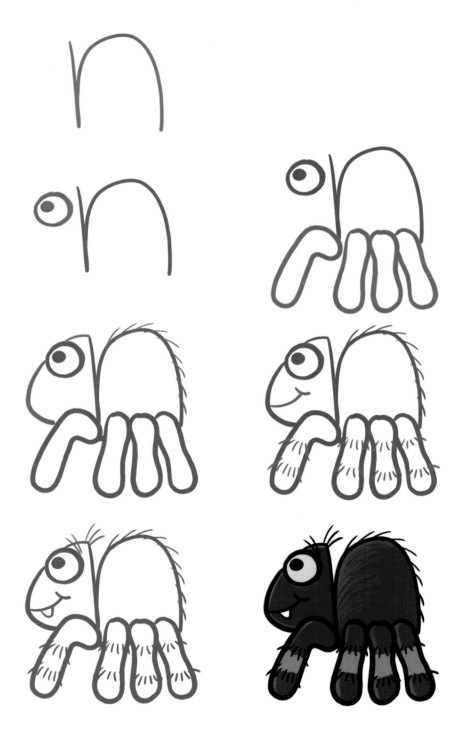

capybara

chinchilla

Watch Steve draw this at
HowToons.com

mini pig

BY STRETCHING THE CIRCLES INTO DIFFERENT SHAPES YOU CAN MAKE ALL KINDS OF PIGS.

hedgehog

Watch Steve draw this at

pygmy goat

miniature horse

Dress your Pet

HERE ARE SOME FUN IDEAS ON
HOW TO DRESS YOUR PETS.

TOP DOG

BASEBALL CAT

NINJA GUINEA PIG

COSMIC CAT

TRY DRAWING SOME
CRAZY PET COSTUMES.
JUST HAVE FUN!

ALLERGIC TO FUR?
DRAW A ROBO PET.

CAN IT EVER GET TOO
WEIRD? NO WAY!

Visit Harptoons.com and watch how-to-draw videos, print off FREE coloring and activity pages, and create fun crafts. Mail your drawings to Harptoons.com and you might see it in featured in the Art Show. All this and more at the greatest drawing site dedicated to getting young people drawing, creating and imagining.

Follow Harptoons on: